# Hard Luck

## by

## Mary Arrigan

First published in 2007 in Great Britain by
Barrington Stoke Ltd
18 Walker St, Edinburgh EH3 7LP

www.barringtonstoke.co.uk

ISBN: 978-1-84299-448-1

Printed in Great Britain by Bell & Bain Ltd

# A Note from the Author

When I was fourteen our English teacher took my class to see a play by Shakespeare. We chattered and giggled all the way to it. My best mate Joan and I lagged behind everyone else. At the corner of the street where the theatre was, a boy stood and watched us all. We were laughing and having a great time! He asked Joan and me where were we all going.

"To the theatre," Joan said.

"Wow!" said the boy. "That's dead nice, that is."

"*Dead nice*," we giggled to each other and we ran to catch up with the rest of the class.

And the play really was "dead nice". Real actors and actresses made the story come alive. It wasn't like the Shakespeare play we'd had to read in school. When we left the theatre, we saw the same boy again. He was sitting in a doorway with a dirty blanket around him.

"Was it good?" he asked Joan and me when he saw us.

"It was brilliant ..." I began.

"Come along, you two," our teacher shouted. I looked back at that boy. I'll never forget his face. He so wanted to hear what it was like to see a play in a theatre. Was that something he'd ever get to do himself? I don't think so ...

For Duncan
*And in memory of my uncle,
Joseph Nolan,
Shakespearean actor*

# Contents

# Chapter 1
# Leaving Home

Rain. You can stuff newspapers and bits of cardboard inside your coat to help keep out the cold, but you can't do anything about the rain. It seeps right into your clothes and down your neck. Every step makes your trainers squelch. Your trousers get cold and wet and rub against your legs. You might find a railway bridge or a truck that's parked up for the night. Then you can stay out of the rain for a bit. They give great shelter. That's heaven, that is. Having some shelter is just great.  You can curl up against one of the bridge walls or behind a truck's big wheel.  Then you can listen to the rain's slip-slap.  You feel safe because none of those drops can get to you.  But if another person has got there before you, it can all end in a fight.  So if there is another person there, you're better off keeping away and pushing off into the rain again.

I'd been out since early morning.  When I say early morning I mean around three o'clock.  That was when Bill came home.  He was Ma's new partner.  Ma wasn't really my mum.  I'd been fostered out to her from the children's home when I was six.  She got money every month for that.  It was OK when she was with Rob.  He was laid-back and we did fun things together.  But he left when I was eleven.  And now there was Bill.  Ma met him in the pub where she worked as a cleaner.  At first he was OK too.  Didn't bother me much. He made fun of me for going to school but that was all.

"Nancy boy," he'd laugh. "Off to your naff school, eh? Never did anything for me, school. Never needed it. Got where I am today without any of that stuff."

One day I got fed up with his remarks. "Like being able to sign on is something to brag about?" I said. "Get a life, Bill. All you do is sign on to get money for booze and then you just sit around like a dosser all day."

That was the first time Bill hit me. A stinging slap right across my face. It hurt. I could cope with a slap. I know what you're thinking. You think I must have had a death wish when I talked back like that to a loser like Bill. But I'd got so fed up with the way he filled up our house with bad moods and fights. I just had to say something.

Life had been OK when it was just Ma and me. But she wasn't the mumsy sort and she only kept me on because of the money she got for fostering me. She didn't care who knew that. She spent the day in bed, smoking fags until it was time for the pubs to close. That's when she'd go to work. We didn't meet much. That was fine by me. I could cook myself some eggs and crash down on the sofa to chill. Comfort.

But then Bill came along. By day he just hung about and got in my face. Then, when it was time, he'd go to the pub. He'd stay there until Ma finished her cleaning job. Mr Jones was the pub landlord. Bill told him he was there to escort Ma home after work. Bill said the streets weren't safe so late at night. But I knew that was just an excuse for him to stay on drinking.

After that first fight things got bad between me and Bill. The next time I annoyed him he hit me again. And that's how it always was after that. He always hit me where the bumps and bruises wouldn't show. I fought him off. I'm no coward, me. At first Ma tried to stop him. But then she didn't bother any more. That's when I felt it was time to go.

I took all the books out of my school rucksack and packed as much as I could into it. Jumpers, socks and all that. I had some money hidden in my pillow. It was all still there. I counted it. Sometimes Ma or Bill found where I'd hidden my money. It was the cash I earned for stacking shelves in the corner shop on Saturdays. Then they'd nick it.

Last of all I picked up a class photo of our school trip to London with our English teacher, Miss Waters. That was the best day of my life. We went to a play called *A Midsummer Night's Dream* in a big theatre. Miss Waters was always talking about the theatre.  She had lots of friends who worked there.  That school trip was great.

I had no idea what a live play would be like.  It just blew my mind.  I wanted it to go on forever.  The words the actors used ... it was like listening to soft music and eating honey and melted chocolate all at the same time.  And the way the play looked – the stage – it was pure magic.  All flowery woodland and trickling streams.

Afterwards, we had to write about it. Miss Waters read my work out loud.  I blushed and looked around in case anyone called me poncy.  But no one did.

After that, Miss Waters made a big effort to help me.  She gave me books to read.  Bill ripped one of them up in a rage one day.  I couldn't believe it when I saw the torn bits of paper float to the floor.  *Flitter, flitter.*  I wanted so much for Bill to die.  What would I tell Miss Waters?  But she didn't mind.  She said that people could rip books up, but they could never rip the words out of your head.

I really liked Miss Waters. She made me feel special. That's why I put the photo into the inside pocket of my coat. It would help me remember the short time I got real respect.

It was odd when I shut the front door. I had shut that door every day for years. I knew the *thunk* it made as it bumped over a broken tile that had never been mended. Tonight was different. I waited for just a moment before that last *thunk*. I tried to think of some reasons to stay, but there weren't any. I pulled the door shut and took a deep breath of the cold night air. I'd never felt so alone. *Thunk.* The door shut. I'd done it. I was on my own now.

# Chapter 2

# Miss Waters

Wet plastic bags blew along the side of the road like lost ghosts. Every now and then the bags stopped still and then their shapes changed and they moved on again. You look at things like that when you're alone on the streets. I kept in the shadows. There was no point in standing out. I'd be asking for trouble.

At the Tesco car park I found shelter under a truck. Of course I checked first that there was no one else with the same idea. I knew about junkies who crash down anywhere and turn nasty if they're disturbed. There wasn't anyone there. That was good. I made my rucksack into a pillow, then I snuggled down as best I could.

I watched the rain as it drizzled in circles around the street lights. If I watched that drizzle long enough, maybe I'd fall asleep and then I'd forget all the bad stuff in my head. I did fall asleep but the bad stuff stayed in my head. My dreams were all about falling down holes. And when I woke up I knew the dream was telling me something. When I'd left home, I'd done just that – fallen down a deep hole.

Perhaps if I snuck back now I'd be home before Ma and Bill got back. Perhaps I should just get on with my life at home and wait until I was 16. Then I'd be free to leave. That was only a year and six months away. Could I live in the same house as Bill for one year and six months? Perhaps Ma would put things right. Maybe she'd even dump him. Nah. That wasn't about to happen. So I put my head back down on the rucksack again and waited for morning.

It was the noise of cars that woke me. 8.30. I took a deep breath. I began to panic then. In the wet light of day what I'd done seemed so stupid.

People were beginning to arrive at the Tesco's to shop. I rolled out from under the truck and brushed myself down. And then I slapped myself on the head. I'd forgotten to pack any food. Idiot. I looked over at the lights of the supermarket. It would be warm in there, and if I was lucky there might be some free samples of food to try out on the stands. I smoothed down my hair at the doors. *Swish, brr.* I was in.

"Why, Matthew, you're out early this morning," I heard someone say.

I had that panicky feeling again. But I quickly told myself that I'd done nothing wrong. I was just another early morning shopper. I fixed my face back to normal and turned to see who'd spoken to me. It was Miss Waters.

"You're getting your shopping done before school, just like me," Miss Waters said with a laugh. "I wouldn't have thought you were someone who got up so early."

I hunched my shoulders, and stared down at the clean floor. There weren't many shoe marks on the floor tiles yet.

"Is your mum here?" Miss Waters went on and looked all around. I knew she'd like to meet Ma. Ma had never gone to the parent-teacher meetings.

"No, Miss Waters," I muttered. "It's just ... just me. Just here to pick up a few things on ... on my way to school." I added that because Miss Waters would know I couldn't get home with the shopping and then get to school on time.

"Ah, then you'll want a lift. Meet me back here in five minutes and I'll take you. No need for you to hoof it when both of us are going to the same place."

I had no choice but to wait. I couldn't tell Miss Waters what was really going on or let her think I was on the dodge.

She came back  a little later. She'd done her shopping and she'd got me a coffee.

"I'll bet you didn't have much time for breakfast," she grinned. "Get that down you while I check out this lot."

Now I was glad I'd waited. That coffee just warmed me right down to my toes. I helped Miss Waters load her stuff into her car.

"Thanks, Matthew," she said. "You can just put the shopping on the front seat. I find it easier to unload from the front seat. Maybe you won't mind sitting in the back, eh? Did you get your own shopping?"

"Hadn't much to get." I nodded quickly. "Just lunch."

As I lifted the bags into the car, I couldn't help seeing the things she'd bought. Things like fruit, French bread, real vegetables, and wine. And I thought about what it would be like to live in a peaceful house where you could enjoy that stuff and talk to someone about interesting things.

"Just push that sack across," Miss Waters said as I climbed into the back seat. There was a black plastic sack on the seat and it fell over when I pushed it. Some clothes fell out and I began to stuff them back in. "I'm dropping that lot off at the charity shop after school," she laughed. "Doing a big clean-up at home. You wouldn't believe the mess there is, Matthew."

No, I wouldn't. Miss Waters didn't look like a messy person. I wanted to tell her that my house was *really* messy. But the words didn't come. She might ask about our mess and I'd have to make up a lie. I couldn't tell her about the beer bottles, cans and takeaway boxes all over the house.

"This is nice," I said as I stuffed the last thing back into the bag of stuff for the charity shop. It really was nice. It was a quilt – an old bedspread, the sort you'd see in films about long ago. All the squares were neatly sewn together. There were flowery ones, stripy ones, and silky ones. Miss Waters looked back at me in the driving mirror.

"Oh, that. It's been around for ages. There comes a time when you have to let things go, Matthew. *Feng-shui* is all about dumping mess."

I hadn't a clue what she was talking about, but I smiled like an idiot and nodded.

"It's dead nice," I muttered.

"You can have it if you like," she went on, and looked back at me in the driving mirror again.

"I can?"

"Of course, Matthew. I'd like to see it go to someone I know. Leave it in my car and pick it up from me after school."

How could I tell her I wasn't going to school? Not ever. I had that panicky feeling again. What had I done?

"I'll take it now, if that's OK," I said. "Thanks very much."

"Won't there be rude comments if you arrive in school with a quilt, Matthew?" Miss Waters asked.

"No one will make rude comments," I said. "Not unless they want a fight."

Miss Waters gave a funny sort of laugh. "Have it your own way," she said. The car turned down the road to the school. Panic again.

"Miss Waters," I said, "if you don't mind I'd like to get off here."

She gave another laugh. "I understand, Matthew. You don't want people to see you coming to school with a teacher. That'd be asking for trouble."

"Something like that," I muttered, as I rolled up the quilt and opened the car door.

"Take care, Matthew," said Miss Waters. "See you later."

I so wanted to tell her what I was doing. But I knew I couldn't. What could she do? She'd have to report me and then Ma and Bill would get me back.

"Miss Waters ..." I began to say.

"Yes, Matthew? Have you changed your mind?"

I stopped. Did she know what I was thinking? I couldn't speak.

"About the quilt," Miss Waters went on. "Do you want to pick it up from me later?"

"Oh. No, I'll hang on to it. I just want to say thanks," I said.

"You've already said thank you, Matthew."

"Well, just ... thanks for everything," I muttered.

"What a gentleman you are, Matthew."

Gentleman. Gentle man. I had to laugh.

"It's true," Miss Waters said, her face serious. "And don't you forget it," she went on. She began to drive away. I had that feeling again – that I wanted to tell her everything. Then the moment passed and I stood and watched the car head off down the road. I put the rolled-up quilt under the straps of my rucksack and headed away.

# Chapter 3
# Nowhere to Go

That evening I hung around outside a chip shop. I wasn't brave enough to go in. That's just daft, isn't it? I'd been going into shops and chippies for food for years. There was never much left for me at home. When I'd started working at the corner shop, Ma stopped giving me my lunch money. At first I just got my lunch with my own money. But soon all the money I'd saved up was almost gone and I snapped at Ma. I told her I'd report her because she wasn't feeding me properly. That did the trick. It made me feel good too. Ma knew that if I did report her she'd be in trouble.

After that she gave me as little as she could get away with. It wasn't ever enough, but I'd make it last as long as I could. In fact Mr Fusco, who owned our local chip shop, got to know me. He'd slip in some fish or a burger but only charge me for the chips.

This time was different. I was miles away from Mr Fusco's shop and I was on the run. What if Ma had reported me to the police by now and they were on the look-out for me? What if I met someone who knew me and grassed me to Ma?

I'd just made myself go into the chip shop when two guys pushed into me. One wore a hoodie that hid most of his face, and the other wore a baseball cap right over his eyes.

"Move it, kid," the hoodie said as he thumped the quilt on my back. That was Miss Waters' quilt. It was my last contact with someone who mattered to me. The guy with the hoodie made a fist and thumped the quilt again. I hated him for that and I started to feel scared.

"Back off," I hissed, and I pulled away from him. He looked hard at me. His thin mouth was a straight, angry line. He pushed me again and I fell outside. He moved towards me and I got ready for a fight. His pal looked back and laughed.

"Come on, Tono," the pal said. "Too early for fun."

The Tono guy in the hoodie gave me a nasty grin and went up to the counter with his friend. I waited until they sat down at a table before I went up to the counter myself. The smell of burgers and chips made me forget about the two guys. Food! I fished my roll of cash from my pocket and counted out enough. I was going to treat myself – cheeseburger, chips, a bun and a milkshake. I was so hungry I didn't care how much money I spent.

I sat at a table near the window and looked out at the grim street outside. It was raining again. Passers-by blurred into dribbly shapes. They leaned against the wet wind as they walked along and held onto their coats to keep warm. Cars and buses splashed by. It was five o'clock. People going home from work. *Home.*

I almost said the word aloud as I thought about what sort of homes people were rushing to. They'd be going into warm houses where other people said, "Hello, glad you're back," and asked about their day. I was being soppy now. Maybe it was because the café felt cosy and safe. Home. It's funny how a word can just come into your head and take over.

I bit into the burger and thought about my food. But that word – *home* – just kept coming back. *You have no home, you have no home*, my thoughts said as I ate. I shook my head. *What a loser!* I thought. *I can't let thoughts like that get to me now.* I wiped the goo off from around the nozzle of the tomato ketchup bottle and squeezed a small lake of it onto the side of my plate. I dipped each chip and took small bites. That way I could stay longer in the café where it was warm.

There was a clatter of chairs from the other side of the café. Tono and his friend were going. That was good. It didn't bother me at all when Tono made a devil sign at me with his fingers. They were going and I was safe here. I still had the bun to look forward to.

It was getting quite dark now. The streets were a bit emptier. There was room for the sheets of rain to dance on the wet pavement. How nice it would be to sit here on the inside all night. But the bun was almost gone now. I felt cold inside. It was getting dark and I had nowhere to sleep.

# Chapter 4
# Mugged

"You're going to get that sleeping bag mighty wet, kid," the chip shop man said as he saw me at the door. "Here, let me give you something to cover it."

He dug around under the counter and found a black plastic bin bag.

"This will do the job," he smiled. He helped me wrap it around Miss Waters' quilt. "Nice sleeping bag," he went on. "Are you going camping?"

"No, I ..." No words came. My mind was a blank. I didn't know what to say.

"Look, kid, none of my business, eh? I don't need to know. I've got enough to think about. Just ..." He stopped and looked at me. "Just be careful, OK?"

I nodded and headed for the door. The bin bag made rustling noises as I moved. I didn't look back, not even to thank him. I knew if I let him be kind to me, I'd end up telling him my sad story. And I couldn't stay tough and strong and protect myself.

I pulled my collar up around my mouth and tried to shrink down as far as I could into my coat. Fat lot of good that did. The rain dripped into my hair and down into any gaps left between me and my collar. I spent a lot of time standing at shop windows. I'd blow on my hands and look in the windows.

People who saw me might think I wanted to buy the things in the shop – the fridges, cookers, sofas, plasma TVs or trendy clothes. But I wasn't looking at those things. I could see the reflections of the people passing by behind me – like looking in a mirror. That's what I was watching when I spotted a couple of cops chatting and I moved on quickly. But I didn't run. I didn't want the cops to notice me. *Wimp*, I said to myself. I hadn't done anything wrong. No crime. I wasn't about to hurt or mug anyone. So what was I afraid of?

I knew why I was afraid. I was a vagrant now, a tramp – one of the hundreds of people with nowhere to go. I saw other people like me, bent down under damp sleeping bags or raggedy blankets in the doorways of shops that were shut for the night. If I looked at them, they didn't look back at me. They were trying so hard to be invisible. Just like me.

God, I was so worn out. It's hard to go on and on walking down dark, wet streets. When the rain stopped, I sank onto a bench under a tree. Would anyone see me if I slept there? If I just closed my eyes for a few minutes I'd get the energy I needed to move on again.

"Well, lookee here."

I jerked awake as two bodies sat down with a bump on both sides of me. It was the two guys from the café – Tono and his friend. They pushed up against me so I couldn't move.

"Not going home to Mummy tonight, then?" said Tono. "Little boy like you shouldn't be out so late, should you?"

"Dangerous, that is," the other guy roared in my ear, making me jump. They both laughed.

"What do you want?" I growled. I kept my voice low so they wouldn't see I was afraid.

"What do we want? He asks what do we want," Tono snarled.

"We want your dosh," said his friend. His grinning face was hidden under his baseball cap.

"I have no money," I said. I tried to shake the two of them off me.

Tono leaned so close his face was just centimetres from mine. He grabbed my collar and pulled me even closer. "Lies, you little creep," he sneered. "Where's that nice roll of dosh we saw you with in the chip shop?"

"We'll just have that, if that's OK with you," put in the other guy.

"NOW!" Tono yelled in my ear. "We don't like waiting, me and my friend Otis here. Come on, Otis," Tono hissed.

Otis took out a knife and I knew I had no chance. Sure, I could put up a fight – I can defend myself OK if I have to. But I knew with these two, it was no good. I'd end up hurt and bloody. And I'd lose my money as well.

"Get off me, if you want my money," I growled.

"OK, OK, my man," laughed Otis. "Up, Tono, and give the kid some room."

Why had I been so stupid and kept all my money together in a tight roll? As I felt in my pocket, I wished I'd kept some money in my bag or somewhere else. Then I could have held on to some of it. Now I had to hand over everything. I looked around for some passer-by to come and help me. But no one looked over at us. No one ever stops for three guys with a problem between them.

Tono grabbed the money and smelt it.

"Ah," he said. "I love the smell of warm money."

I was desperate. But at least Tono and his friend would leave me alone now. I was wrong. Otis pointed to my quilt.

"That's another nice roll," he said. "I like that roll. Warm and comfy. You like that roll, Tono?"

Tono grinned. "Yeah," he said. "I think we should have that. And maybe the rucksack too. We might as well take the lot, huh?"

I gritted my teeth.

"Back off," I muttered. "You've got all my money. What more do you want?"

"I *said* what we want," said Otis. He put the knife right up to my chin. "C'mon. Hand them over.  We got better things to do, me and Tono, than argue with a wimp."

I didn't care about the rucksack, but there was no way they were going to take Miss Waters' quilt away from me.  I pulled it off the rucksack and held it close, kicking out when Otis tried to grab it.  But there were two of them, and a knife.  After a few seconds they'd knocked me down and made off with everything I had left.

# Chapter 5
# The Old Man

The man who tripped Otis up wasn't big.
He was tall, yes, but thin and gangly. One
moment he was walking towards us, swinging
a walking stick. Then, with a quick flip, he
turned his walking stick upside down and
caught Otis's ankle with the crook of the
stick. With a jerk he put the thug on the
ground. His foot pressed down on Otis's
throat, and he simply held out his hand and
took my rucksack and the quilt from him.
Tono waited just for a second. Then the man

swung the upside-down walking stick at him. Tono could see that the man's foot was still pressed on Otis.  Tono ran.

*So much for sticking by your buddy*, I thought as I ran over and grabbed my stuff. By now there were some other people around as well.  Two men in tracksuits dragged Otis to his feet and held him tight. A woman with a dog got out her mobile and rang the police. More came along to see what was going on. *Where were all these people when I was being robbed?* I thought.

Then a police car pulled up and I began to back away.  I didn't want to hang around for the police to question me.  But I needed to know that they'd get Otis.

The old man put his walking stick over his arm and put his hand on my arm.  "Don't you want to give evidence?" he said.

I looked at him.

"You don't want to get involved, is that it?" he said.

I nodded.

"That's OK," the man went on. "There are enough other witnesses to give evidence. He won't get away."

We slipped away softly, the old man and me.

"That was a good thing you did," I said. I tucked the quilt back into the straps of my rucksack. "Thanks, mister."

"Hmm. Sorry I was too late to get the other guy," he answered. His voice made me feel better. It was posh and low. Someone with a voice like that could solve all problems. The old man went on, "I expect the guy I caught will tell the police about his pal in any case. They'll both get done. Did they take anything else?"

"He got my money," I muttered.

"Oh, too bad," said the man.

"Nah. Doesn't matter. This is more important," I went on, patting the quilt.

"Has it got more money sewn into it?" the man asked with a smile.

"I wish," I said. "No. It's ... it's just a quilt."

We were now back on the street. The man turned towards me. For an old man he was tall and straight. He wore one of those Australian hats that you see in films. His coat was long and it swung round him as he walked.

"You look like you could do with a cup of tea, lad," he said, looking down at me.

"No, thanks," I replied. "I'm fine." I didn't want to get involved. When you've just been robbed, you get a bit nervy round people you don't know.

The man smiled. "I can understand," he said. "Why don't we just go to a café where there are other people? Then you can get up and go whenever you like. How does that sound?"

"No," I said. "I ... I have to be off."

"Train to catch? OK. Nice meeting you. Cheers."

I watched him as he strode along the street into a warmly lit café. I was alone again. I had to spend another night on the streets. And I didn't like it.

*The man has helped me out*, I thought. *He seems nice.*

Yes, but so do lots of weirdo murderers look nice. Weirdos who make friends with loners like me. They invite them home and then kill them for the fun of it.

Still, that café looked warm and cosy, and I felt so worn out and cold. I'd been out in the dark for six hours now. And the man *did* say I could get up and go any time I liked. And there were plenty of people sitting at tables. The old man could hardly strangle me in front of them, even if that was his plan.

I stood outside for a moment. My wet jeans stuck to my legs and my socks were cold and damp. I needed to dry out and warm up. I went into the café.

# Chapter 6
# Charm

The old man looked up and smiled when I put down my rucksack and pulled out a chair. He didn't laugh at me.

"Tea, is it?" he asked, and lifted his hand to call a waitress over to the table. I nodded. "How about a sandwich?" he went on.

"That'd be good," I muttered.

As he gave the order I looked him. His silver-grey hair was long – it came to just below his chin. He had a short beard. That was also silvery grey, a bit yellow round his mouth from cigarettes. His coat had looked smart in the dark outside, but in the light inside it looked shabby. The Australian hat, which was on the table, had a greasy mark around the brim. He had a tartan scarf round his neck over a grubby blue and white check shirt. His fingers were long and elegant. And, as the old man bent towards me, I got the smell all down-and-outs have. Was this man someone posh who was living on the streets for fun, or had he fallen on hard times, like me?

The waitress went away and the old man looked hard at me.

"You didn't want to stay and give evidence, then," he said. It wasn't exactly a question, more of a statement.

"Huh?" I didn't get it.

"When the police arrived," the old man went on, "you didn't seem to want to hang around to give evidence."

"Well," I answered, "you didn't seem to want to hang around yourself, remember?"

The man smiled. "You've got me," he said. "So, neither of us wanted to chat to the police. You have your reasons and I have mine."

If he was waiting for me to tell him what my reasons were, he'd have to wait. I was keeping my mouth shut. I played with a paper napkin and ripped it into little bits. He didn't ask any questions and we just sat in silence. The waitress came and set out cups and saucers before us. I looked up at the man when she was gone. His face was still, a half- smile on his lips as he gazed around the full café.

"Sometimes," he said, "it's nice to be part of the human race. But only sometimes."

He was starting to freak me out now. But when the waitress came back with a pot of tea and two sandwiches, I thought I'd take my chances and stay put. I could get up and go any time.

"Ham," said the man. He nodded at the sandwiches as he started to pour the tea. "One ham and one egg – because I never know whether my dinner guests eat meat or not."

I looked up at him again. Dinner guests? Was he loopy or what? I put my hand out for the ham sandwich.

"A meat-eater then, eh?" he laughed. "What say you that we split these marvellous offerings and have one ham and one egg sandwich each?"

"Fine," I muttered. I bit into the soft, delicious mix of bread, lettuce and ham.

Never again would I ever take food for granted.

The hot tea went right down to my cold, damp feet. I began to relax. I just wanted to stay here all night in the warm.

The man sniffed his cup of tea. "This tea," he said, "is like dish-water. I sometimes despair over what's being done to elegant living. Excuse me, my dear." He waved to the waitress. "I would be so grateful if you would bring my good friend and myself some boiling water."

The waitress gave him an eager-to-please smile. Why? Was it the man's good manners or his posh voice? She nodded and went to get the water.

I couldn't help grinning.

"Charm, my boy," said the man, and he turned towards me again. "Always remember that charm moves the hardest of hearts."

"Like, if I had used charm on those guys who mugged me, they'd have given me back my money and some of their own as well?" I said. "Get real, mister."

The man threw back his head and laughed a deep, musical laugh.

"Point taken," he said. "Let's just say that you have to choose with care who you wish to charm."

What with the tea and feeling warm again I began to relax. Here was someone who was happy to talk to me as if I was his friend. And, when he held out his hand and said, "My name is Jeremy," I shook his hand and said, "I'm Matthew." That was all. No surnames. They weren't important.

# Chapter 7
# Under the Bridge

"Now, Matthew," Jeremy said as we mopped up the last bits of egg from our sandwiches, "the time has come to pay our bill. What I want you to do is go outside and wait for me one hundred metres down the street to the left of the café, OK? One hundred metres, no more, no less. Understand?"

I began to speak, to tell him that I was heading for ... nowhere. But that wouldn't make much sense. So I just nodded. I pulled my rucksack and rolled-up quilt back onto my back. Then I looked back at him as I opened the door. He sat at the table, looking relaxed. His long legs were crossed and one elbow was on the table. He didn't look at me. What was I to do? Well, I didn't want to be on my own on the streets again. I took a deep breath. I'd take my chances and wait for Jeremy. I'd be very careful. I'd make sure we stayed where there were plenty of people. So I plodded along to where I thought one hundred metres away from the café was, and waited.

I felt as if I'd waited for hours, but I think it was only about fifteen minutes. Time seems much longer when you're hanging about on a street. Then, just as I was thinking Jeremy would never turn up, he came running down the street. He ran with great lolloping steps. Without stopping, he tapped me on the back and made me gallop along with him.

"What ...?" I began.

"Shush. Don't waste time with words. Just keep running, boy."

And so I kept on along with him until we reached the grotty end of town. Jeremy stopped, leaned on a wall by the river and took deep breaths.

"What was that all about?" I asked.

Jeremy took off his hat and rubbed his sleeve across his face. "It's rather hard luck," he gasped. "Hard luck, Matthew, that I find myself a tad short of money just now. It was a case of making a quick exit while I asked that kind waitress to fetch me more hot water. An old trick I learned ..." He stopped to catch his breath.

"You mean you didn't pay?" I asked. I felt shocked but I had to admire his cheek.

"Something like that," he muttered. "Now tell me about yourself. You *are* running away, of course."

My mouth opened and shut like a gold-fish in a bowl. "How did you know that?" I blurted out. Then I saw how I'd fallen for his trick. I could have kicked myself. I should have thought for a second and come up with a better answer. He knew about me now.

"Yes," I muttered. "But I'm going to be OK. I'll get a job in a supermarket and get on with my life."

Jeremy shook his head. "How old are you, Matthew?" he asked.

I started to add a few years to my life, but when I looked at Jeremy's old, grand face, I couldn't lie.

"Fourteen," I mumbled.

"Fourteen.  And what's the first thing they'll ask a fourteen-year-old when you go to look for a job?"

I shuffled a bit.

"You haven't really thought about this, have you, Matthew?  Even if you do ask for a job in a supermarket, they'll want your birth certificate, address and all your details.  It's the law.  They have to do that."

"I'll get by," I said.  "I'm tough, me."

"Of course you are," said Jeremy.  "So tough that it took an old geezer like me to pull you out of a nasty spot.  You'll do well, lad."

"Now you're making fun of me," I said.

"Just a little," he answered.  "Look, Matthew, let's think this over.  Come with me ..."

"No!" I said, backing away. "I don't know who you are. Just because you bought me tea and a sandwich doesn't mean you own me."

"Don't you mean *nicked* tea and a sandwich?" he laughed.

"Whatever. Just ... just leave me alone, OK? I've got to go."

"Whatever you like, lad. But remember that if you change your mind I'll be under the bridge over there. There are others like me there. We look out for one another. You just ask for Gentleman Jeremy and they'll find me. *Au revoir.*"

For the second time that night I watched him go away from me. He went down some steps and vanished under a dark arch. *On my own again*, I thought. I could cope. I could do this.

I sat up by the wall and watched the dark river ripple past. In the glow of the street lamps I could see the first raindrops make a pattern on the water. Looking up, I could feel those raindrops on my face. The rain was getting worse. It was past midnight and a rainy night was ahead of me.

I couldn't take any more. There'd be no harm in having a look at where Jeremy was – but I'd be ready for a quick getaway. So I went down the steps where he'd said good-bye and made my way along to the bridge.

As I got nearer the arch, I could see a glow of firelight. I kept in the shadows and peered in. People were standing around a fire that blazed up from a barrel. Jeremy towered over them as he stopped to chat. There was laughter and then he was gone. I didn't want him to vanish. Suddenly I felt very alone. I wanted to warm myself at that fire. I wanted to be part of the laughter, to belong. I went up to where the fire was.

# Chapter 8

## *Chez Jeremy*

Heads turned as I got nearer to the group. They huddled closer together. I could sense they didn't want me there. But it was too late now to turn back.

"What you want?" a woman's voice called out. "You get outta here. This place is none of your business."

A short man took a burning branch from the barrel and held it up towards me.

"You heard the lady, mate," he shouted. "Now git, ya hear?"

I held out my hands. "I'm ... I'm looking for someone," I stammered.

"Yeah, right," another voice said. "The only 'someones' here is us and we don't know you, so beat it."

The man with the flaming branch started to come towards me, his face red and angry in the firelight.

"Jeremy," I said quickly. "Gentleman Jeremy. That's who I'm looking for."

The man stopped and looked back at the others.

"Who's askin'?" the woman asked. She rubbed her hands together and went to stand beside the man with the branch.

"Matthew, missus," I said. I remembered what Jeremy had said about charm. "He knows me."

The woman shouted out to one of the people behind her.

"Frank! Tell Gentleman Jeremy he has a visitor."

We stood watching each other and no one moved. We waited for Jeremy. He took one look at me and welcomed me as if I was an old friend.

"It's all right," he said to the group as he led me past them. We went towards a line of broken-down old shelters made up of cardboard boxes, tin sheets and wooden crates.

Jeremy pulled back a grubby curtain and, with a grand bow said, "Welcome to *Chez Jeremy*." I ducked and went inside.

"*Chez Jeremy*" was simply two large wooden containers pushed together.

"Lounge," he said pointing to the one on the right. "And Master Bedroom on the left. You, my friend, will sleep in the Lounge."

There was only just enough room for the two of us to sit on the scruffy cushions that were scattered on the floor. There was a table made of an old tray on a stool. A camper stove with a frying pan on it stood in a corner. A couple of mugs and a tin plate with lots of dents in it were stacked on an upturned plastic basin.

Jeremy didn't ask me any questions. I was just there and he was happy with that. I didn't say anything.

"I would offer you tea," he said. "But we have just had dinner, you and I. So I'll wish you goodnight. Do turn off the lamp before you go to sleep."

Lamp?  I looked around, but all I could see was a single candle in a chipped mug.  I smiled.  I was getting used to Jeremy.  As he got up to go I felt a bit nervous.  He must have seen it in my face because he nodded in at the group outside.

"No worries about my neighbours," he said softly.  "We're a mixed bunch who go our own ways, but we have to protect this dry spot of ours, here under the bridge."

And, with that he closed the curtain and I was on my own.  As I wrapped my quilt around me, I felt like a king in a palace.  What more could anyone ask than a warm place to rest and a friend to share it?  For the first time since I'd closed Ma's front door, I really slept.

# Chapter 9
# Hopes and Dreams

Over the next few days I stopped worrying about Jeremy. I wanted to ask him so many questions. Why was he living rough? He was so posh and grand, I couldn't understand. But I didn't ask. He knew where to get soup from the charity workers late at night. He knew which restaurant back-doors to go to for leftovers. He told everyone I was his good friend, Master Matthew. That made me laugh. And I hadn't laughed for years. In fact, the first time I laughed Jeremy smiled and asked where I'd left my scowl. *Back somewhere I wanted to forget about*, I wanted to say. But I didn't tell him anything about myself yet.

One morning Jeremy looked me up and down.

"We need to do something about how you look, young sir," he said. "Today we're doing culture."

"Huh?"

"The National Art Gallery, my boy. We're going to visit the National Art Gallery. Free, warm and marvellous. Have you ever been?"

"Course I haven't," I muttered. "But I was at a play once." I grinned. "That's culture. *A Midsummer Night's Dream*, it was called. I even have a photo. Right here in London. So there, Mister Smarty – have *you* ever been to a play in a real theatre? Ha!"

Jeremy didn't laugh. In fact, for just a few seconds he looked upset. And when I began to tell him the story of the play he shook his head and held up his hand to stop me. I laughed and said, "Shakespeare too good for you, huh?"

But he looked back at me and smiled. "Come and meet my tailor," he said.

His "tailor" was a woman who worked in an Oxfam shop.

"This is Madam Browne with an E," he said and kissed her hand. "Now," he said to her, "I've brought you a young gentleman who is in sore need of good clothes."

The woman who was *Mrs Browne with an E* smiled. "You old charmer," she said. "Let me see what I can do."

"I'm not going to wear a soppy suit or something," I whispered. "I don't do that stuff."

We settled for a Nike jacket and jeans.

"Put it on my tab, dear lady," said Jeremy.

"Just go, Jeremy," she said. "Before I get into trouble."

And so we went to the National Art Gallery. Just for an hour. Jeremy said that it was better to take a bit at a time at an art gallery than gallop through the whole lot of paintings.

"You enjoy a little at a time, Matthew," he said. "If you try and see everything all on one day, the paintings get mixed up in your head. We'll come back again."

That night we sat in a shopping centre and talked about the paintings. Stressed-looking people whizzed past with bags and trolleys. As Jeremy talked to me, I saw life in a different way. I learned to think about things I hadn't thought were important before.

One evening, as we walked over the bridge, Jeremy stopped to look out over the river. "Tell me, Matthew," he said. "What level are you at now?"

"Huh?" I said. "You're talking rubbish, Jeremy. Levels are to do with computer games, man. Not something you know much about."

"I mean level of life," he said. He looked at me and his face was serious. "You have got to a better level than where you were when you ran away. What's next? What are your hopes, your dreams?"

I shook my head. "You ask some weird questions," I laughed. "I don't have hopes or dreams. I'm ... I'm now. This is where I am."

Jeremy shook his head. "You're a drop-out forever?" he said. "A tramp? A vagrant who lives in a box with a washed-up has-been and a bunch of down-and-outs? No, dear boy. You are a bright young man. You must have dreams."

I gave a shrug. "What's the point of having dreams? I'll never get anywhere with them," I said. "I have nothing, Jeremy, and I expect nothing ..."

"No!" Jeremy looked at me sharply. "That's the voice of defeat. You must never listen to the voice of defeat. You must make things happen. You're the only one who can do that for yourself. Only you." Then he turned back to the river. "Even rivers go on to somewhere better," he said softly.

I wanted to react. What were *his* dreams? Why was *he* down on this level? Why didn't he have somewhere to live? But I could see he was thinking about something and wouldn't answer my questions.

We didn't get back to the National Art Gallery again. When we went back to our shelter that night our world fell apart.

# Chapter 10

# Homeless

We knew something was wrong the moment we saw the arch ahead of us. There was no fire, no talk. The darkness was silent. We crept towards the arch without making a sound. Then someone flashed a torch at us. We froze.

"What the hell is going on?" said Jeremy. He put his hand up to his eyes because the torch was shining right at us.

"Oh, it's you, Gentleman Jeremy," someone said.

"What's going on?" asked Jeremy. He marched towards the torch.

"The council," the man said. "They must have come in the afternoon when we were all away. The others have gone. What's the point in hanging around, eh? No point in staying around when the council are doing a clear-out. Scum!" he spat.

"Lend me your torch, mate," said Jeremy. His voice was shaking a little.

He shone it around. Where our "home" had been, there was now just a pile of broken wood and scraps. All our belongings were in an enormous skip next to it. I had a sick feeling in the pit of my stomach. How could anyone do that to the scraps and comforts of a few homeless people?

"Quickly, Matthew," said Jeremy. "Grab anything you can. We must get away from here. Once the council move in, the police will be watching that we don't move back."

His voice scared me. I found my quilt down at the bottom of a pile of ragged blankets and old curtains. I grabbed it. I looked around for my rucksack, but that was gone.

Jeremy found some of his clothes. I wrapped them, along with some socks and a jumper of my own, in my quilt, and I tied everything up with some string I'd found.

Jeremy took one last look around. Even in the torch-light I could see that he was upset. His face was white. He looked worn out.

"Let's go," he said.

That night we slept in a doorway. Neither of us said anything much. What was there to say? What could we say to make ourselves feel better? The home we'd felt safe in was gone.

We spent our days sitting in parks if it was sunny, or in stuffy shopping centres when it rained. Jeremy had no energy any more. He seemed sad and tired when we went to the restaurants he knew to ask for left-overs.

"Why don't we find a hostel?" I said, one cold night. "If we get there early we might get a couple of beds ..."

I broke off as Jeremy shook his head. "Not for us, my boy," he said. "At least, not for me. I'd prefer to breathe the night air than try to fight vagrants who are off their heads on drink or drugs."

"But at least we'd be in out of the cold," I argued. He still shook his head.

"I've been," he said. "Once, when I first ..." He broke off again. "When I first opted out," he added at last in a low voice. "One time in a hostel was enough, Matthew. But don't let that stop you. If you wish to try it, then feel free. Your choice. Anyway, it's time you moved on. You can't hang around with me forever. Go and tell your story to social services. Get sorted, lad."

I thought for just a moment. "I can't leave you, old man." I made my answer into a joke. "I couldn't bear the thought of you being swept into a dustcart in the early morning clean-up."

One evening it scared me to see Jeremy's white face. He looked so worn out. I wanted to take him to a hospital, but he wouldn't let me. He leaned on me. He didn't even seem to notice where we were going. In the end, I found a dry, sheltered doorway. As soon as we'd settled ourselves, people began to walk past. They were well-dressed people and they'd look at us and then look quickly away, the way people do when they don't want to think about bad stuff. Then I saw where they were all going. There was a theatre further up the street. I watched as they chattered and waited on the street outside.

Jeremy's eyes were shut. I wanted to shake him, to make sure he was OK. He had become everything to me, and now I had to look after him.

"Jeremy," I whispered. "I'm going to see if I can get us some tea. OK?"

He nodded, without opening his eyes. I begged some money for a cup of tea from a man and woman on their way to the theatre. I rushed back to give Jeremy the tea and then I stopped. There was a woman stooping over him. When I got nearer I heard what sounded like angry questions. Why would anyone be angry with a tired old man?

I ran and I spilled some of the hot tea over my hand.

"Oy!" I shouted. "Leave that man alone. He's not doing any harm!"

The woman turned. We looked at one another with shock.

"Matthew?" she said. "Is that you, Matthew?"

# Chapter 11
# Starting Over

"Will he be OK?" I asked one more time. "Do you really think he'll be OK?" It was four months now since that evening when Miss Waters had found Jeremy and me outside the theatre.

Miss Waters laughed. "Of course he will," she said. "Now, hurry or we'll be late." She shut the door behind us. "Here's the taxi."

In the months that had passed since that night when she'd met us, Miss Waters had become my foster mum.  There were still legal things to be settled.  But the authorities had found out what my life had been like with Ma and Bill, and they had been quick to agree I should stay with Miss Waters.  She found me a place in a different school.

"Fresh start and new friends," she'd said. "No hassle over living with a teacher."

I thought about all these things in the taxi.  I could hardly believe how different my life was now.

There was a crowd, of course, when we arrived.  But now I was part of that crowd.  I looked at all those chattering people and then looked back at Miss Waters.  She smiled as she handed in our tickets.  My heart just thumped and thumped as we waited for the lights to go down.  And when that curtain was slowly drawn back, I had to blink several times to make sure I wasn't dreaming.

\*\*\*\*\*\*\*

It was the quilt, of course, that had got me here. That precious quilt. This is how it happened on that night in that doorway.

Of all the people in the world, I would not have wanted Miss Waters to see me living like a tramp. When I saw her looking at me I'd felt so many different things. Then she had come towards me.

"The quilt, Matthew," she said softly. "I saw the quilt I gave you. I needed to know how this man had your quilt."

I began to back away.

"Come back, dear boy." Jeremy spoke at last. "This lady won't hurt you. Hear her out."

Miss Waters turned towards Jeremy. In the street light I could see the amazed look on her face.

"I know that voice," she said.

Jeremy just shook his head slowly. I didn't know what was going on.

Miss Waters took us to a café and ordered a hot meal for both of us.

"Now," she said. "Tell me how you two met up."

Jeremy and I looked at one another. I didn't know where to begin. But Jeremy, with hot food inside him, was back on form. With several cries of "Oh, my goodness!" from Miss Waters and the odd bit from me, we told her how I'd run away from Ma and Bill and how Jeremy and I had met on the night I was mugged.

"What happened to *you*?" she then asked softly as she turned to look at Jeremy. "*You* had it all – every theatre wanted you. Your name was at the top of the posters for all the great plays."

"Huh?" I blurted out.  I almost choked on the bun I was eating.

Miss Waters smiled.  She was still looking at Jeremy.  "This man is Frederick Leyland. He was one of the greatest actors in the country.  And then ...?"  She looked at Jeremy.

I stared with amazement at Jeremy.  He wiped his mouth with his napkin.  I could see he was thinking of what to say.

"Frederick Leyland?" I began.  "Is that your name ...?"

"My stage name, dear boy," he said with a smile.  "I'm still Jeremy to my friends.  Five years ago my life turned pear-shaped," he went on.  He looked at Miss Waters.  "I'd spent too much money, I was drinking too much and the theatres were picking younger actors instead of me.  I felt I was on the scrapheap.  My wife left me.  I lost my house. I had nothing.  So I simply opted out of life.

Not something I'm proud of," he went on.
"But I'd gone so low I thought there was no
turning back.  I'm a washed-up has-been."

If he thought Miss Waters was going to
feel sorry for him, he was wrong.

"Has-been?" she said.  "We'll see about
that.  You'll sort yourself out, mister.  I'll see
to that."

********

Four months on, I know that whatever
Miss Waters says she'll do gets done.  She
always seems to know the right people to
help you out.  After that evening when we all
met up, Miss Waters sorted everything out.
She found a small flat for Jeremy, paid for by
the council.

"It will do until you get back into acting,"
Miss Waters said.

And that's how we came to be sitting in the theatre today. Miss Waters knew some people who worked for the theatre. They'd found Jeremy a new agent and he'd got a small part in a play called *Macbeth*.

When the play began, I could hardly watch. I waited for Jeremy to come on stage. Then it was time. I caught my breath. There was Jeremy. Right there on stage, playing the part of a porter. My friend Jeremy. I wanted to shout and cheer, laugh and cry all at the same time. Miss Waters squeezed my hand and looked at me with a grin. The two people who made up the warm, colourful part of my life were right here with me. My life was just beginning.

Barrington Stoke would like to thank all its readers for commenting on the manuscript before publication and in particular:

| | |
|---|---|
| Lizzie Alder | Bilal Mohammad |
| Carly Baranowski | Danielel Plant |
| Elmer Bottomley | Trudy Puddle |
| Sarah Francis | Christine Phillips |
| Laura Hampton | Saeed Ramzan |
| Daniel Hardwick | Frankie Regan |
| Phil Hassell | Jonathan Seale |
| Imran Hussain | Hannah Storey |
| Susan Kaye | Holly Weston |
| Milo James Manfred Bright | |

## Become a Consultant!

Would you like to give us feedback on our titles before they are published? Contact us at the email address below – we'd love to hear from you!

info@barringtonstoke.co.uk
www.barringtonstoke.co.uk

# Also by the same author ...

# Chocolate Moon

## by Mary Arrigan

Chris's gran is starting to forget things – sometimes it's like she's not there at all. She's got Alzheimer's and it's hard for everybody.

Chris wants to make things easier for her ... but what is the chocolate moon she keeps talking about? And can he help her see it again?

You can order *Chocolate Moon* directly from our website at **www.barringtonstoke.co.uk**

If you liked this book, why don't you try ...

# The Bone Room

## by Anne Cassidy

**Evil from the present, terror from the past ...**

An empty cottage. A cold room. A thing in the chair. Noises under the floor.

Paul and Lulu want to know the truth – but it puts them in danger. Can they stop a terrible crime? And what is the real secret of the Bone Room?

You can order **The Bone Room** directly from our website at **www.barringtonstoke.co.uk**

# If you liked this book, why don't you try ...

# Kill Swap

## by James Lovegrove

A boy with a *big* problem.

A man who says he has the answer.

Darkness. A gun. Somebody about to die.

The nightmare has just become real ...

You can order **Kill Swap** directly from our website at
**www.barringtonstoke.co.uk**